TUCKER
AND THE BEAR

Jane Chambless

TUCKER
AND THE BEAR

SIMON AND SCHUSTER BOOKS FOR YOUNG READERS
Published by Simon & Schuster Inc., New York

SIMON AND SCHUSTER BOOKS FOR YOUNG READERS, Simon & Schuster Building, Rockefeller Center, 1230 Avenue of the Americas, New York, New York 10020   Copyright © 1989 by Jane Chambless   All rights reserved including the right of reproduction in whole or in part in any form.   SIMON AND SCHUSTER BOOKS FOR YOUNG READERS is a trademark of Simon & Schuster Inc.   Manufactured in the United States of America

10 9 8 7 6 5 4 3 2 1

Library of Congress Cataloging in Publication Data: Chambless, Jane.   Tucker and the bear / Jane Chambless.   p. cm.   Summary: Tucker is bothered by the big bear who comes to stay with him, until the bear goes away and Tucker finds he misses his friend.   [1. Bears—Fiction.   2. Friendship—Fiction.] I. Title.   PZ7.C358Tu 1989   [E]—dc19   89-30244   CIP   AC

ISBN 0-671-67357-2

For Ted E.,
the best bear of all

ONCE UPON A TIME, not so very long ago,
there lived a boy named Tucker.
Tucker lived all alone in the forest.

He was very happy there. He had books
to read and he had pictures to draw.

Best of all, he could daydream for hours, and there was no one to interrupt him.

One day, a bear wandered by.

"What a nice house," said the bear. "If you let me stay the winter, I'll help you with your work and keep your house tidy. I'm good at that."

Tucker thought about it awhile.
"O.K.," he said.
   The bear was very big. He took up lots of
room, and Tucker's house was not very large.

That evening, the bear made dinner for Tucker.
All through dinner, Tucker just played with
his food. The bear was not very good at cooking.

When it was time to wash the dishes, Tucker
watched as the bear broke one plate after another
with his big, clumsy paws.
He wasn't very good at washing dishes.

The bear liked to take naps. He would settle down and snore so loudly that Tucker couldn't concentrate on the book he was reading.

When Tucker sat down to draw a picture, the bear would come and crouch behind him and try to peek over his shoulder. The bear got in the way a lot.

When Tucker wanted to take a quiet walk, the bear would follow him—talking all the time.

The bear was not good at being quiet. As hard as he tried, he just didn't seem to be good at *anything*.

One morning, Tucker woke up and found the bear was gone. Outside his house, winter's first snow was softly falling. Tucker looked everywhere, but the bear was nowhere to be found.

"How quiet it is this morning," Tucker thought to himself. "Now I'll be able to read, or draw, or maybe just sit and daydream without any more interruptions."

But as hard as he tried, it was much too quiet to read. Drawing wasn't fun anymore, and his daydreams always drifted back to wondering about the bear.

When he went for walks in the forest,
he missed the bear walking beside him.
Tucker was lonely.

The winter slowly passed.

One spring morning, the bear came back to
Tucker's house.
    Tucker was glad to see his friend again.
"Come in and have breakfast with me," he said.

He made a special "welcome back" feast of pancakes. The bear enjoyed them very much. He had always been good at making a mess.

Tucker was very happy. "Please stay with me, bear," he said. "At last I've found out what it is you're really good at."

"What's that?" asked the bear.

"You're good at not letting me be lonely. You're good at being my friend."
The bear smiled back at Tucker and nodded.

And they both were very happy.